FALLING FOR
HIS MATE

A CRESCENT MOON STORY

Savannah Stuart

Cover art: Jaycee of Sweet 'N Spicy Designs
Author website: www.savannahstuartauthor.com

Falling For His Mate/KR Press, LLC -- 1st ed.

ISBN-10: 1635560233
ISBN-13: 9781635560237

eISBN: 9781635560206

CHAPTER ONE

"You sure you know what you're doing?" Sybil asked as they cruised down the main strip of Orange Beach, Alabama.

Andrew just grunted. Mainly because hell no, he wasn't sure. But he was second-in-command of the O'Shea pack. He had to appear to be sure, all the time. Normally he never second guessed himself. He'd also never fallen for a she-wolf before. Yeah he'd had shifter lovers, but Charlie… he'd fallen hard for her. Then he'd screwed up.

"I'll take that grunt as a big fat no. And that you're a dumbass."

He jerked in surprise and glanced at her in the passenger seat. Tall, with long curly auburn hair, she was definitely one of the beauties of his pack. Not that she did anything for him—and vice versa. They were more like siblings. "Dumbass?"

Sybil lifted a shoulder.

"Okay fine. Maybe I am."

"There's no maybe about it. And let me tell you something, even if you get her to forgive you, you're going to have to get her wolf on your side too. If you'd ghosted on *me* like that? Dude, my wolf would claw up your face on sight. On principle."

"I know." He was a wolf shifter too, so of course he knew. They weren't like humans. Their dual nature was part of their DNA, who they were. So the reminder that the female he'd fallen hard for might attack when she saw him? Yeah, not fucking needed.

"It's gorgeous down here," Sybil said a few minutes later.

"Yeah." Orange Beach in early May was definitely that. It was pushing noon, the sky was blue with a few streaks of white scattered overhead. Not that he cared. All he wanted was to get to Charlie. "This is it," he said, slowing as they reached the turnoff to the Kincaid pack 'compound'. His heart rate increased a fraction. Soon he'd see Charlie again.

For the next few weeks, or however long it took all the alphas in the southeast region to meet and discuss potential alliances and what to do about the rash of rogue vampires that had been infiltrating their territories, this was his and Sybil's home. Each alpha had traded a couple of their packmates with other packs.

It was difficult for any alpha to leave their territory unprotected, so they'd come up with this trade of sorts. The logic was that no one was going to attack another pack because if they did, the packmates they'd traded would be killed. Only a shitty alpha would put his own people in danger. And the packs meeting all had strong, honorable alphas. This was just a failsafe to keep everyone in line. Andrew had volunteered, which was strange for a second-in-command to do, but his alpha had let him. Even though it had put their young pack at a disadvantage. He'd needed to see Charlie in person, to apologize. To make things right.

"Pretty sure I'm going to be down here visiting again," Sybil said as he steered into the now opening gated entrance. "I wish we lived closer to the beach." There was a wistful note in her voice.

The Kincaid pack had beachfront property and every member of the pack had an ocean view. According to what he'd learned, each condo was the same size—except the second's, who lived in the penthouse. The alpha had his own home right next door to the condominium complex.

As soon as he'd parked and they'd stepped out of the vehicle, Andrew felt multiple sets of eyes on them. He might only be in his thirties, which was young compared to a lot of the pack members here, but he was still alpha in nature. As second-in-command, he had extra honed senses.

Before they'd taken two steps, Max McCray appeared from the bottom floor of the complex. With icy blue eyes that promised death if he stepped out of line, the male was no one to be messed with. Neither was he. Andrew might be in another pack's territory, but he couldn't be anything other than who he was. And he was not submissive, in any sense of the word.

Striding forward, Andrew nodded and held out a hand to the male who was over a hundred years old. His scent reminded Andrew of the beach in winter. Nothing like Charlie's scent—which was wild blueberries and peaches. Nope. He locked that thought up because if he started down that road, he'd get a hard-on. And that was just embarrassing. He'd been in control of his body since he was a pup. Ever since meeting Charlie, however, his entire world was off its axis.

Something he'd sworn would never happen. He'd seen the way his father was completely whipped by a female, the complete imbalance of their relationship. That was never going to be him. Or that had been the plan.

But here he was. In Orange Beach because he couldn't stay away from a dark-haired female with eyes the color of melted chocolate and a scent so wild and free it unleashed all of his primal instincts. Instincts he hadn't known he even had. As a wolf he was more in touch with his primitive side than his human side on the best of days, but she'd brought out something untamed inside him.

"How was the drive?" Max asked, looking between the two of them.

"Good." Uneventful, which was all he could ask for. He quickly glanced around, taking in the high wall. From the main road he hadn't been sure, but now he could see that the high wall surrounded the entire place, giving the pack complete privacy. And not totally out of the ordinary in gated communities.

"This place is gorgeous," Sybil added. "And I heard your pack has a private pool."

Max half-smiled at her. "Yeah. Lauren's off today, waiting to show you around. Threatened an important part of my anatomy if she wasn't off when you got into town."

Andrew snorted as Sybil laughed. Lauren was Max's jaguar-mate and Sybil had become friends with her the last time Lauren had visited with their own alpha's mate—who was also friends with Charlie.

"Good. She promised me a beach day."

"You guys have a lot of bags?" Max asked as Andrew opened the hatch to the SUV.

"Nah." Andrew hauled out Sybil's overpacked suitcase and his own small duffel bag. What the hell she had in here, he couldn't imagine.

"I'll show you to your rooms. I've got you in separate guest condos. I didn't have any next door to each other, but if you want—"

"We're good with whatever you've given us. And thank you for the hospitality. We also want to offer to help out wherever is needed. I know you're out two packmates right now." Well, four technically, since the alpha and his mate were also away at the treaty meetings.

Max simply nodded as they reached the stairs.

Andrew was glad they were taking them instead of the elevator. His wolf needed to stretch and expend energy. He hoped for a run tonight on the beach, but needed to check with Max about that first. His own pack had enough private property that they could run free whenever they wanted. But this was a different territory with different rules. And a very different terrain.

It didn't take long to reach the fourth floor and when they passed one of the condos, he scented wild blueberries and peaches and nearly stumbled.

Charlie.

The scent was old enough that he knew she wasn't nearby, but it still lingered in the air, the smell more potent than anything else in the long hallway. This was her floor.

And since the hallway was completely glassed in, instead of wide open, it would contain scents longer. He swallowed hard, willing his body under control. Her scent shouldn't affect him so strongly, but his wolf had gone over a month without seeing her, touching her, smelling her... Hell. They'd never even gotten naked together.

Not that he hadn't thought about it—and fantasized about her every night while he used his fist to take the edge off.

A few moments later Max opened a door only four doors down from Charlie's place. The male motioned that he could go inside. He also said some other stuff, but Andrew couldn't focus on his words because all his wolf could think about was hunting down Charlie, marking her, claiming her.

He rolled his shoulders once and dropped his bag in the kitchen as Max said, "You'll be on security at one of the hotels or at Crescent Moon Bar—unless you'd like to help out at the salon instead." He said the last part almost jokingly.

Which told Andrew that Max didn't know about what had happened between him and Charlie. Because she owned the salon. He cleared his throat. "Salon's fine with me."

Max straightened slightly. "You sure?"

Out of the corner of his eye, Andrew saw Sybil fighting a smile. "Yeah."

"We're a progressive pack," Sybil added, not bothering to hide her smile now.

Max glanced between the two of them, shrugged. "Fine. I'll let Charlie know you'll be helping out tomorrow. She's the owner and in charge there. So whatever she wants you to do, you do."

The thought of Charlie telling him what to do, ordering him around should have rankled him. He was too alpha for that. But... it oddly didn't. Even if she clawed him up, he just wanted to see her. Hold her.

"I can just call her myself," he said neutrally. "I'm sure you've got a lot on your plate with your alpha gone."

Max nodded absently as he glanced at his phone. It had buzzed half a dozen times since he'd met them in the parking lot. "Yeah, okay. I'll text you her number. Sybil, I'm going to show you to your place, then I've got a few fires to put out."

Andrew didn't tell the other second that he already had Charlie's number. No, he just waited until Sybil and Max were gone before he allowed his canines and claws to spring free.

Fuck, fuck, fuck. His body was his to control. Always. But right now, knowing Charlie was so close, his wolf was agitated and beyond listening to reason.

Somehow he managed to force his claws to retract long enough so he could strip out of his clothes. Then he let his wolf take over completely.

Fur replaced skin and for a few moments he was the most vulnerable he'd ever be. It was always like that during a shift. Pleasure and pain mixed together as his primal side took completely over.

Panting, he trotted around the condo, sniffing everything as his beast calmed down. Letting the shift take over was the only thing guaranteed to help him relax.

And he needed to be calm when he went to see Charlie. Because no way in hell was he texting her, giving her a warning that he was on his way. If he did, she was likely to be gone when he got there. Or maybe not because she was the kind of she-wolf to face things head on. She'd more likely just punch him. Either way he sure wasn't waiting until tomorrow to head to her new salon.

No, he'd be dropping by this afternoon. Because he had to see her. To apologize to her. And hope that he could convince her to give him a second chance. The thought of giving up his role as second, the pack that he loved… it was hard. But he couldn't stay away from Charlie anymore. She was his to claim.

CHAPTER TWO

"You look fantastic," Charlie said to Anna, one of her human clients. In her forties, the woman was kind, elegant and always trying new things with her hair. She was one of Charlie's favorite patrons.

"You speak the truth." Grinning, Anna stood. "These caramel highlights are great, and just in time for summer." She ran her fingers through her long, mostly dark hair. "My Jorge is going to love it."

Charlie was pretty sure Jorge didn't care what Anna did because the male was so in love with her. They'd been together since they were eighteen, had two wonderful kids and every time Anna spoke of her husband, the sweetest scent rolled off her. Even when she was annoyed at him, the scent of her love for him was clear. It made Charlie adore her even more. "Also true. You want to set up an appointment now, or text me later?"

"Later," she said, rising from the chair. "Not sure how long I'll keep this style."

Charlie took Anna's cape and draped it over the chair. She'd only been open six weeks but she'd been doing Anna's hair for years. One of her side businesses that she'd finally decided to turn into something bigger. With so many built in customers, Charlie's opening had been successful. "I'm betting a month," she said as she held out her phone and credit card magstripe reader.

Anna swiped her card and grinned. "We'll see."

After talking for a few more minutes, Anna left, the bell jingling overhead as the door closed behind her.

"I heard the new traded packmates are here." Erica stepped out of one of the private rooms they used for massages, eye lash extensions and waxing.

They were careful never to talk about anything pack related in front of humans. At best, people would think they were crazy. At worst... There was a reason the supernatural world kept their existence a secret from humans. The humans couldn't handle it. Not yet anyway. Maybe one day. Charlie sure hoped so anyway. It would be nice not to have to hide her dual nature. But humans liked to worry about too much stuff; like what other people did in the privacy of their bedrooms. It would be a while yet until they could deal with the reality of shifters and vampires.

"Yeah?" Charlie had called her friend Alyssa, curious about who would be sent from the O'Shea pack, but her friend hadn't returned her calls or texts. Which wasn't like her, but Alyssa would have been prepping for the upcoming alpha meetings with her mate. Not to mention she had a ton on her plate in general. Still, a part of Charlie wondered if it was because *he* would be coming down to Orange Beach.

But no, Andrew was second for the O'Shea pack. No way would he be down here. They'd need him to take care of everything in their territory while the alpha couple was gone. Which was good. Because she didn't want to see his stupid ass anyway.

His stupid, very fine ass. Gah. He was almost a foot taller than her, but she wasn't blessed in the height department, so that wasn't saying much. At five feet three inches, most of her pack towered over her. Well, except her jaguar packmates. Since they'd joined, at least she wasn't the only shorty.

"Yeah… what are *you* thinking about?" Erica held her broom at her side and eyed Charlie carefully.

"Nothing."

Her friend snorted. "Yeah right. You just got the weirdest look on your face. And your scent is weird too. What's going on?"

Charlie's scent was probably crazy because when she thought about Andrew Reid, she got turned on and pissed off simultaneously. Her emotions went haywire and neither her human nor wolf side had any control. She hated that the male made her feel unbalanced. It had been like that since the moment they met.

"Oh, look alive. Sexy male walking inside in five, four, three..." Erica went back to sweeping up the cut hair.

Charlie turned toward the door, not because she cared about the sexiness factor, but because she had a job to do. All thought fled her mind the instant Andrew sexy-as-sin Reid stepped into her salon.

Against her will, she sucked in a sharp breath. His dark hair was a little longer than it had been the last time she'd seen him. He still had that sexy beard and even though she hadn't thought the whole 'lumberjack' look was hot before him, he pulled it off. The male looked as if he should be cutting down trees and carrying off the trunks in one arm. With broad shoulders, icy blue eyes that at one time had captivated her... Nope. Nope. Nope. Absolutely not going there.

"What the hell are you doing here?" she snapped before she could stop herself. *Great. Way to play it cool, dumbass.* Gah. She'd sworn to herself that if she ever saw him again she'd act unaffected, calm. Too bad her wolf had other ideas. And right now, her wolf wanted to claw up his handsome face. She resisted the urge to unleash her claws. Barely.

"Hey, Charlie." The quiet baritone of his voice flowed over her like warm honey. Just like his dark but sweet scent. Like honey and chocolate.

She wanted to claw him up for that too—his scent shouldn't be a freaking aphrodisiac. But it was. And she wanted to roll around in it, cover herself in *him.* "What do you want?" Okay, she couldn't even be civil, damn it. Not with this unwelcome surprise. It didn't matter that she'd thought about how she'd react if she ran into him again, the truth was she didn't want to see him. It hurt too much. She'd thought Andrew was different, that what they'd shared had been serious, going somewhere.

She heard Erica hurrying to the back. Not that it would matter, her packmate would be able to overhear everything anyway. Which was exactly why Charlie couldn't have a conversation with Andrew here. Wolves were notorious gossips, which was why she'd kept her personal business with Andrew just that, personal. She was glad, because when he hadn't shown up to her salon's opening, her packmates would have felt sorry for her—and she'd have been the topic of gossip. Something she always wanted to avoid. If her family had known she'd had a broken heart they'd have coddled her, treated her with sympathy—and brought her tons of food. The wolf way to heal a broken heart. The food part would have been all right, but everything else? No thanks.

"You look good," he murmured, taking a few steps closer.

"I know I do." And of course, so did he. She kept that thought to herself. "Now what. Do. You. Want."

He cleared his throat and glanced around curiously, or maybe nervously. But she couldn't imagine him being nervous about anything. He was the one who'd decided to cut her out of his life, not the other way around. "I'm here as part of the trades," he finally said, meeting her gaze again.

It took a moment for his words to compute in her overtired brain. "But you're the second-in-command." Okay, way to state the obvious. She inwardly winced.

He lifted one of his oh-so-broad shoulders, his gaze never leaving hers. "I'm sorry for ambushing you, but I wanted to let you know I was in town."

"Well now I know, and now you can leave."

He winced slightly, but really, he shouldn't be surprised by her reaction to seeing him. "Ah, I'll be helping out at the salon."

No scent of a lie rolled off him and really, why would he lie about that anyway? Gah.

She tightened her jaw, then unclenched it, forcing herself to breathe normally. "Well we're about to close. No more appointments for the day, but we open tomorrow around nine." And she was going to talk to Max long before then and make sure that this jackass was moved to a different duty. No way was she letting him work here, in her domain. Even if she did need the help since two of her packmates were in O'Shea territory—and one of them worked here.

"Can I take you out for dinner? Or a drink? I was hoping to talk to you." His expression was so hopeful, she wasn't sure what to think of it.

Before she could answer, Erica came out from the back, her purse in hand. "Hey, boss. I was thinking of dipping out early. Will you be okay without me?"

Charlie eyed the leftover hair on the floor, but knew that Erica wasn't shirking her duties. No, Erica was one of the hardest working wolves in the pack. She was trying to give Charlie privacy, and Charlie knew her friend was one of the few wolves who wouldn't run off and gossip about this. "Yeah, I'll be good. Thank you." She injected a wealth of emotions into those last two words, wanting her friend to know she was grateful.

Erica nodded once and bared her teeth at Andrew as she passed him, a growl low in her throat. Charlie blinked in surprise, then bit back a grin. Her packmate might not know what was going on, but it was clear enough that Charlie wasn't a fan of Andrew. As Erica left, she flipped the OPEN sign to CLOSED.

Without looking at Andrew, more for her sanity than anything else, Charlie headed to the front door and flipped the lock into place. "I've got to run end of the day reports and since you ran off my packmate, you get to sweep. The hair vacuum will suck it all up. Just sweep it in front of it," she said, motioning to the small vacuum built into the baseboard.

Wordlessly, Andrew did as she ordered. His scent and presence were driving her crazy. It was too surreal that he'd be working with her for the duration of the alpha meetings. And it made no sense. Why the hell did he want to take her to dinner? To see her at all? He was the one who'd disappeared from her life as if what they'd shared had been nothing to him. As if she didn't matter.

Did you send the O'Shea second to work at my salon? she texted Max as she started running her numbers in the back office. She had a cash deposit she needed to make today, and after she finished here, she'd be able to head out.

Yeah. He requested it. That a problem?

Charlie debated her answer as she digested the news. Was Andrew trying to mess with her head? She stared at her screen for a long moment. If she said yes, then Max would want to know why. Because Charlie was easy-going and the fact of the matter was, Andrew was a guest in their pack's territory. No way was she going to make waves and draw attention to herself by requesting that he be transferred. Even if she'd planned to do just that. No, she needed to play this cool or the entire pack would be sniffing around her, wanting to know what had happened between her and Andrew. *Nah, just wanted to double check with you.*

Sounds good. Let me know if it doesn't work out and I'll move him somewhere else.

Thanks, Max.

"All done." Andrew's voice, far too close for comfort, made her jump. She looked up from her desk and glared at him. There was barely a foot of space between them and her office was the size of a matchbox. She only used it for business and admin stuff.

"You're in my personal space." Her voice was surly and completely unlike her. Which just made her even madder.

He took a step back, his expression neutral. "I finished sweeping. What else can I do?"

She nearly snorted. She wanted to be rude and tell him he could leave, but she bit her tongue. She had to get herself under control. This wasn't her and she didn't like being this emotional ball of anger. "Nothing," she said, turning back to her laptop. "I'm just about done here." After saving the reports and grabbing the deposit envelope of cash from the lockbox in her desk, she stood.

"That's all you need to do?" His expression was dubious.

No, she could clean up a bit more, but she'd just come in early and do it. Right now she needed to get away from him. Not to mention she'd promised a packmate she'd cover a shift at the Crescent Moon bar tonight. It meant she'd be working a long double shift, but that was okay. Whenever she needed someone to cover for her, a packmate always stepped up. So after her deposit, she was headed straight to the bar.

"Yep." Snagging her purse, she headed to the front door, with Andrew close on her heels.

His scent wrapped around her, practically smothering her as she set the alarm. It started beeping, letting her know they had forty-five seconds to get out.

The cool salt-tinged breeze rolled over them the second they were outside, and she inhaled deeply. The smell of the ocean always soothed her, centered her wolf. The scent of the mountains did the same thing. Her wolf was pretty much satisfied when she was outdoors, getting fresh air. Of course, not right now. Nothing could take the edge off.

As soon as she locked the door and turned to face Andrew, it was as if the breath was stolen from her. Her chest squeezed for a moment as she looked up, up, into those clear blue eyes.

"Please have dinner with me," he murmured, his gaze dipping to her mouth. The hunger there jolted some sense into her. "I'd like to talk."

He didn't have a right to look at her like that. He'd lost the right. And there was nothing to talk about. "I can't. We open at nine tomorrow. Be here if you want." Turning from him, she headed to her Jeep. Once she was inside and had a certain amount of distance from him, she sucked in a full breath.

And realized he was still standing in front of the salon's door, watching her. Damn him. Double damn him! She slid her sunglasses on and started the engine. Time to get out of here and away from him. She could only hope that the alpha meetings were over as soon as possible.

Then he'd be gone and out of her life for good. Even if she didn't want to make waves, if it was too hard to work with Andrew, she'd have to request that Max move him.

Because even if she wanted to appear unaffected, she wasn't. Simple as that. Andrew had hurt her. Deeply.

Earlier in the year she'd gone to visit her friend Alyssa in South Carolina for Alyssa's baby shower. Andrew had stopped by the alpha couple's house and for the first time in her life, she'd understood what it meant to experience fireworks inside her.

Their gazes had collided and she'd felt that connection all the way to her core. It would have been embarrassing if he hadn't clearly been just as bowled over by her. She barely remembered their first conversation, just the way he'd made her feel. All hot and bothered. Charlie had extended her stay, telling her pack that she wanted to help out Alyssa with baby stuff. Of course no one had questioned her.

In reality, she'd stayed to spend more time with Andrew—who'd started hardcore courting her. The shifter way. They'd gone on dates, learned about each other, agreed to be exclusive to each other, gotten very physical—no sex at least.

Things had seemed great, though a part of her had been worried that she'd only been getting surface stuff from him.

As if he'd been holding back. Turned out he had been. Because everything between them, their connection, had been a giant lie. Because the Andrew she'd known wouldn't have promised to come to the opening of her new salon, then just ghost on her.

When he hadn't shown up and then hadn't returned her calls, she'd started to get truly worried. Until she'd spoken to Alyssa—who'd told her that Andrew was fine. He hadn't been injured, or off on top secret pack business. Nope, he'd just decided not to show up.

The reality had been more than a slap of ice water in her face. It had cut deep. Still did. She'd thought they had a connection… maybe even the mating connection.

Obviously not, because mates didn't treat each other like that. So whatever stupid feelings she had for him, she was locking them up tight and burying deep. No way was she trusting that male again. He'd had a chance and he'd lost it.

CHAPTER THREE

Andrew tugged his jeans on over his hips, and buttoned them up before pulling his shirt on. Next came the shoes, something his wolf hated. But he was about to enter a civilized establishment. Well, sort of.

Crescent Moon Bar was shifter owned, but it wasn't supernatural exclusive so humans would be there too. Sybil had mentioned the bar to him and since there was no way in hell Charlie would be talking to him tonight, he'd packed a small bag, shifted and gone for a run along the beach until he reached the beachfront bar. According to Kincaid pack rules it was okay to run along the beach at night, especially when it was hazy out. And there had been no visible moon tonight.

Unlike some human lore, shifters changed whenever they damn well pleased, regardless of the moon's phase. Most wolves looked more like big dogs anyway when running in shadows so he hadn't been too worried about being seen.

The beat of the music from the bar and restaurant filled the air. Not loud enough to offend his extra-sensory abilities, thankfully. Shifter bars and other establishments were like that. Music was at a normal decibel, not ear-pounding obnoxiousness.

As he stepped onto the boardwalk that led from the beach to the restaurant, his shoes were silent along the wooden planks. The breeze from the Gulf kicked up, rolling over his arms and for a moment, he scented wild blueberries and peaches.

It almost paralyzed him, just like the first time he'd seen Charlie. She was petite and adorable and he liked their size differences, liked how she fit perfectly up against him when he wrapped his arm around her. He liked everything about her.

The first time he'd ever taken her out was etched into his mind. He'd known then that he was a goner. But he'd been stupid enough to try to fight what he knew without a doubt was the mating instinct. He'd bailed on her after making a promise—after telling her that he'd completely fallen for her. Because he'd been a coward. And mates or intended mates didn't break promises.

He rolled his shoulders once as the memory of the first time he'd taken her out assaulted his mind.

Like a randy pup, Andrew had to contain his canines as he jogged up the steps of his alpha's home. A place he'd been in too many times to count. Tonight was different, however. Tonight, he was picking up Charlie.

A female he'd met that afternoon at Alyssa's baby shower. Talk about being knocked on his ass. Charlie's long, dark hair had been in a single loose braid draped over her shoulder, covering one of her full breasts. She'd been wearing a snug sweater and black pants with high-heeled boots. And that sweater should be illegal. Hell, everything about her should be.

He hadn't been able to think, much less breathe as their gazes locked. Then he'd just grinned at her, like some fool. She'd smiled right back, at least. As if she couldn't stop herself either.

The front door swung open as he reached the top step. In a red sweater dress and knee-high black boots, Charlie stepped out, a wide smile on her pretty face. "I probably shouldn't admit it, but I've been waiting for you," she said as she pulled the door shut behind her.

Her words slammed into his solar plexus. There would be no mind games with this female. Thank God too. He wanted something real. "Good. I've been counting down the seconds until I could pick you up." He took her hand in his, all his wolf's edges soothed when she slid her fingers between his and fell in step with him.

"So what are our plans for the evening? According to a certain she-wolf, you have no game and she was a little worried you wouldn't know what to do with a female."

He stopped in his tracks, stared down at Charlie in surprise. "Alyssa told you that?"

"Uh, no. Can you imagine her ever saying something like that? I'm just messing with you." She grinned again, a little dimple appearing in her left cheek and it took all his restraint not to lean down and kiss it.

Because if he started and she was into it—and he was certain she would be—he wouldn't stop. They'd end up fucking right on the front porch. "Well, I don't know about game, but there's a movie showing at the drive-in later. I wanted to take you downtown first." His pack lived in a quiet subdivision on the outskirts of a small, thriving town in South Carolina, and he wanted to take her around the historical downtown area first. He wanted her to like it here. So much so, it scared him a little. She was part of another pack, just visiting here. He shouldn't be thinking of the future, but when he looked into her dark eyes, that was what he saw. Their future.

Together.

"Sounds good to me," she said as he opened the passenger door of his SUV for her.

"Favorite type of food?" he asked as he slid into the driver's seat. He wanted to know every single thing about her, right down to the color of her nipples. But that wasn't something he could just come out and ask. He hoped to find out soon though.

"If I had to pick... Italian. I'm addicted to pasta and cheese." She made a little humming sound of appreciation he felt all the way to his dick. "What about you?"

"Same."

"Are you messing with me?"

"No. It's my favorite. But I need meat too. Not just the pasta."

She laughed lightly. "What's your favorite dessert?"

His gaze dipped to her mouth once before he turned back to the road. Thankfully this drive was familiar to him, because he wasn't seeing anything. "I'm pretty sure I haven't had it yet." Because once he got a taste of her... He shifted slightly in his seat and didn't miss the punch of desire that rolled off her.

"You're very bad for my intentions."

"What intentions are those?" he murmured as he turned down a quiet side street not far from a local Italian place that served the best shrimp parmigiana.

"To keep all my clothes on tonight." The faint scent of truth rolled off her, overpowered by another dose of potent lust. Her sweet, addicting lust. The smell was like nothing he'd ever experienced, making him light-headed.

She had kept her clothes on that night, unfortunately. He'd been more than ready, but she'd wanted to wait. Which had been fine with him. Whatever she wanted, he wanted to give her.

Until he'd turned into a coward, a male he didn't recognize. Because he'd let garbage from his past cloud his head.

Rolling his shoulders once, he pulled open the side door of the bar and was immediately inundated with scents and sounds. Island music from the speakers, the scents of lust, liquor, perfumes, shifters and humans filled the air. He filtered out most of it as second nature, like all shifters learned to as pups.

Even as he filtered and ignored most of the scents, the wild blueberries and peaches that was pure Charlie slammed into him. This time, it wasn't faint and it overpowered everything else around him. She was *here*. That was unexpected but definitely not unwelcome.

Like a heat seeking missile, his gaze was drawn to the bar—where Charlie was *working*. Frowning, he headed that way. He knew she'd just put in a full day at her salon and now she was working here?

Ignoring everyone around him, he found an empty spot and slid onto the barstool. She was aware of him about two minutes before she stopped in front of him. Despite her neutral expression he could see the tense lines of her oh-so-sweet body. An observer probably wouldn't notice, but all her muscles were pulled taut. Because of him. Something he hated. Something he planned to fix. He was terrified he'd screwed up completely, that he'd lost his shot with her. Because wolves, when they picked a mate, didn't mess around.

She'd changed since the salon and now had on a black T-shirt, pants and an apron. The plain clothes did nothing to take away from her beauty. Her dark hair was pulled back into a tight ponytail. She touched it nervously as she stopped, met his gaze. "What can I get you?"

"You're working a double?" he asked, the question stupidly obvious.

Her eyes narrowed slightly. "If you're not drink-ing—"

"Beer. I don't care what kind." He hadn't planned to see her again tonight. He'd just wanted to run, get a better lay of the land and maybe meet some Kincaid packmates. He definitely didn't want to ambush her again when she working here. He'd already done that once today and sorely regretted it. Even if he hadn't wanted to give her a chance to run away from him, he should have called or texted. Something better than what he'd done.

She moved away before he could say anything else.

Another female bartender smiled once at him as she ducked behind the bar, coming from the direc-tion of the back of the restaurant. "You been helped yet?" she asked. He nodded once but she didn't move away. "You're with the trades?" The question was innocuous enough so that if a human overheard it wouldn't make sense, but also wouldn't raise any red flags in a bar environment.

"Yep. I'm Andrew."

"Sarah. Nice to meet you." She moved on to a human customer as Charlie returned with his beer.

"Thank you. Would you like a menu?" Her tone was disinterested, not exactly cold. But nothing like the friendly, sweet female he'd taken on that first date, had brought back to his home—brought to orgasm with his hands and mouth. And that was his fault.

Something he had to change. "No. Thank you," he murmured, taking the cold beer that she offered him.

She nodded once and moved on to another customer. Even if he wanted to stay, to drink in the sight of the female who'd stolen his heart, he knew it would make her uncomfortable. That was the last thing he wanted to do.

So he took a couple swigs, dropped a twenty on the bar and slid off the stool. Staying here wasn't an option anymore.

He'd just go on another run. It might not change anything between him and Charlie, but it would burn off a lot of pent up energy.

Starting tomorrow, his plan to win Charlie back began. She deserved to be courted and he was going to give that to her.

CHAPTER FOUR

Six weeks ago

As she headed up the front steps to Andrew's house, Charlie wondered what the hell she was doing, whether she was crazy to fall for this male. She'd just come to South Carolina for her friend's baby shower. She hadn't expected Andrew Reid. Nothing could have prepared her for him anyway.

The male was a force of nature.

Now, two weeks later she was still here, putting off returning home because of him. Her salon would be opening soon and she had a ton more work to put into the place. Because she was going to be completely hands on with every facet of getting the salon ready. Her packmates would help of course, but she wanted to be there for everything.

After spending the day with Alyssa, helping out with baby stuff and just having a fun girls' day, she was excited to see Andrew again. The door swung open as she reached it, making her smile. There was no pretense with this sexy, alpha shifter. He might not be alpha in the sense that he ran his own pack, but he was alpha in every other sense.

"Been waiting for me?" she asked, going up on tiptoes as she reached him.

He brushed his lips over hers, growling low in his throat as he wrapped his arms around her and pulled her tight. With her entire body flush against his, she felt all his hard lines and her nipples tightened in re-action. Just being near him, her body reacted.

"You're two minutes late," he said against her lips.

Laughing, she stepped inside with him, inhaling the familiar chocolate and honey scent of him. It gently permeated the air and everything in his home. "Good things are worth waiting for."

Which was part of the reason she was holding off on having sex with him. He mattered to her and she wanted their first time to mean something, be spe-cial.

"True." Taking her hand in his, he led her through the house and into his backyard.

She could hear his packmates in the distance, at various houses nearby. The O'Shea pack lived on the outskirts of their quaint town. They owned an entire subdivision and a surrounding two hundred acres of forest that Andrew had told her they never planned to develop. Even when they eventually would have to move—as all shifters did because they aged slower than humans and their population would continue to increase over time —they'd hold onto the property. She'd gone running in wolf form more than a handful of times over the last two weeks in the forest and loved the freedom of being able to run wild. At home she always had to run at night along the beach in wolf form and to be very careful about humans. Here she had complete freedom.

He immediately led her to a hammock they'd put together earlier that morning. "How good was my idea?" she asked as they climbed into it.

Laughing, he pulled her close to him so that she was splayed out on his chest. No fat on this male. As with most shifters, he was rock hard and she loved running her fingers over the entirety of his body. She laid her head on his chest, savoring this moment because she knew she'd be leaving soon. They'd agreed to be exclusive, but she still had to return to her pack. They depended on her and she had a new business to run. And she and Andrew hadn't ironed out the details of how they were going to work things out.

"So why a salon?" he murmured against the top of her head, idly stroking a hand down her back.

Shivers of delight spiraled through her at the simple touch. All her nerve endings were raw and awake because of him.

She curled into him, throwing a leg over his long ones. "It's been a dream of mine for a while. After I got a degree in business I moved back to Orange Beach and ended up filling in wherever was needed. But I was constantly looking at real estate and when a foreclosure opportunity came up, I told Grant about it. He'd had no idea I was looking and said he would have just bought a property for me but..."

"You wanted to buy it with your own funds, not pack funds."

"Yeah, which probably sounds ridiculous."

"No, I get it."

She shifted position slightly to look up at him. There was a full moon and a smattering of stars out tonight, illuminating both of them. She wanted to memorize every moment of this night with him. "Really?"

"Yeah. This was something you wanted to do for yourself."

"My packmates will still work with me, it'll be pack-owned for technical business purposes, but... I wanted it to be something I found on my own, something I made happen. Something that I could do even without a pack."

He tightened his grip on her. "That doesn't surprise me at all. I did something similar. Bought the auto shop from a human retiring and turned it into a vehicle restoration place for motorcycles."

She was glad it made sense to him. It was important to her that he understood and she wasn't even sure why. She loved her pack and as a wolf shifter would always live with one. It was part of her dual nature—she needed the comfort of being around others like her. But she also wanted something that was just hers. Apparently he did too. "Aren't you just full of surprises."

Grinning, he dropped a kiss on her forehead.

"So do you work on the motorcycles yourself?" she continued when it appeared he wasn't going to expound. She'd noticed he was like that, not often wanting to talk about himself. And while she'd known he had a motorcycle, he'd never mentioned that he worked on vehicles himself. Such a mystery, this male.

"Some. Not as much as I'd like. I'm busy with pack stuff more often than not." He said it so matter-of-fact, no sigh or anything to let on that it bothered him. And she doubted that it did.

That was the way it was when you were second in a pack. So much responsibility. "Yeah, Max is like that too. I wonder how he has time for his mate most days." Max McCray, the second-in-command of her pack, was always putting out fires. Her alpha was even busier. It was basically impossible to run a successful pack without having a solid second. An alpha always had to have someone they could implicitly depend on.

"I've completely fallen for you," Andrew suddenly blurted, his entire body going tense underneath her after he'd spoken.

Surprise filtered through her at the nervous scent rolling off him. "Right back at ya, big guy." Moving again, this time she completely straddled him, her knees digging into the netting of the hammock as she sank down over his fully erect, unfortunately covered, cock.

The relief that covered his hard features surprised her. It was unbelievable that he could have any doubts as to how she felt about him. She'd extended her stay here because he'd asked her to and though she wouldn't admit it out loud, she was waiting for him to ask her for more. Because if he asked, she'd stay forever.

The thought terrified her but only because she'd be giving up her pack, would have to move her business—one she hadn't even gotten started yet. But for Andrew, all he had to do was ask. He was kind, giving, incredibly sexy but more than anything, her wolf had recognized what he was to her almost immediately. Her mate. She didn't want to say it or even think it, because okay, it was a little scary. What if she was wrong and… no, her wolf wasn't wrong.

And he had to be the one to make the move. The dual part of her nature demanded that he chase her, claim her, mark her. It was simply who she was. While she might not be a beta or submissive, she still wasn't an alpha like him. And she-wolves enjoyed being charmed and chased. At least this one did.

"Do you care if your packmates overhear us?" she murmured, lifting her shirt over her head.

His pale eyes went pure wolf, the animal staring back at her with crystal clarity, and she knew he was beyond speech when he simply growled low in his throat. Using supernatural speed and a kind of agility that impressed her, suddenly she was flat on her back on the hammock and he was the one straddling her.

At the hungry gleam in his eyes, heat rushed between her legs. And all thought fled her mind. He had a way of making that happen, this wonderful, sweet male who'd completely swept her off her feet.

* * *

Charlie bit back a sigh as she shut the door on that fun memory and opened the door to her condo. Or she tried to banish the memory, but it was hard to. Andrew had somehow managed to go down on her in the hammock—bring her to a toe-curling orgasm, then they'd ended up in the grass where she'd done the same to him. As a she-wolf, inside or outside didn't matter to her. She was comfortable with her nudity and sexuality, and definitely comfortable with his.

Gah. No. *No thinking about him.*

Thankfully he'd left the bar earlier and she'd been able to have a decent night at work. The big downside of him temporarily living in her pack's territory was that she scented Andrew everywhere now. In the stairs, in the hallway outside her condo... wait, *inside* her condo. Frowning, she shut and locked the door behind her. No one was here, she was certain of it, but she could still scent him nonetheless. That honey and chocolate scent was faint, but it shouldn't be here at all.

Slipping off her shoes by the front door, she moved quietly down the hallway, following the scent to her bedroom. She smelled... candles? Frowning, she moved to her bathroom and found her big tub was filled and when she tested it with her hand, the water was warm, almost hot. Little tea-lights flickered all around the rim, some on mirrored settings, making the room even brighter.

She stopped when she spotted a white note taped to the mirror over the sink. *This doesn't make up for anything, but I'm sorry. When you're ready, I'd like to talk. –Andrew*

She read the note again, more confused than ever. She also wondered how he'd gotten in here, but it wouldn't have been that hard. She hadn't bothered arming her security system and he was a resourceful male. Though it was impressive that the water was still warm. He must have slipped out mere minutes before she'd gotten home.

However he'd pulled this off, she wasn't stubborn enough to ignore a hot bath after the long day she'd had. Heck, it was technically Friday morning since it was pushing two o'clock.

Yep, she'd be enjoying this bath. And totally not thinking about Andrew or his long fingers and how they'd... no. *Nope.* She needed to scrub her brain of all those sexy images and memories. Pretty hard considering they weren't that old. And so freaking hot they were seared into her memory bank.

Still chastising herself, she quickly stripped and stepped into the bath, sighing in appreciation at the wonderful, wonderful warmth enveloping her body as she slid deeper.

The bath couldn't silence her thoughts, unfortunately. What the hell did his gesture even mean? She knew he wanted to talk, to apologize, but she couldn't imagine anything that would make it okay for the way he'd ghosted on her. Because he'd done it once. What would stop him from doing it again?

Groaning, she ducked under the water, fully immersing herself. Andrew was apparently determined to drive her insane.

CHAPTER FIVE

Charlie felt better prepared for work today since she knew Andrew would be showing up. And okay, she might have dressed up a little. Instead of her normal flats, she'd worn heels that made her calves look even more toned and a blue and white summer dress that showed off all her curves. Simple but sexy. The shoes would kill her feet today, but it would be worth it.

Taking a deep breath to steady herself, she got out of her Jeep, not surprised she was the first one there. Her first client wouldn't be here for another fifteen minutes so she had time to set up. As she stepped up to the front door, keys in hand, Andrew appeared around the corner as if from nowhere, making her almost jump.

Gah, of course he looked delicious. As always. Smelled the same too. Glad that she still had her sunglasses on so he wouldn't be able to see that her eyes had gone wolf, she nodded once at the box of donuts he held in one hand. "You'll be a hit with those today."

He gave her a tentative smile that made her stomach do flips. "I only want to be a hit with you."

She paused at his words then unlocked the door, trying to ignore the honey and chocolate scent of him that overpowered the donuts. She wanted to ask him about the hot bath he'd left for her last night and what was going on with him, but knew that Erica and two others would be here in a few minutes. Not to mention their customers.

"So what do you want me to do today?" he asked, his deep voice wrapping around her just as his scent was.

Her traitorous nipples of course tightened at the combined sound and scent. "Just give me a couple minutes to set up." Even if she'd thought she was prepared for him being here, she'd been wrong. Being this close to him again was a shock to her senses. She was actually trying not to inhale too deeply so she wouldn't go into sensory overload.

"No problem. Oh, I brought you this." He held out the hand with the to-go coffee cup, giving it to her. "It's the way you like it."

She took a sip and a moan slipped free. She'd overslept longer than normal and hadn't had time to make coffee. This was heaven. It was a double latte with a shot of simple syrup—because she loved caffeine and sugar. He'd remembered how she liked her morning coffee. Which didn't exactly surprise her. He'd been incredibly sweet and giving. Until his disappearing act. She hadn't wanted to see him yesterday, and today was even more confusing. She was still hurt by his actions. "Thank you." She started to say more but paused when she saw his wolf in his eyes.

And scented his hunger. Obviously he was in Orange Beach for a reason and wanted to apologize, but to see the raw lust simmering in his gaze took her off guard.

Then he blinked and it was gone. Or at least better hidden.

Clearing her throat, she mumbled something about going to her office before she hurried off, her heels clicking against the tile as she ducked into the back.

Once inside the small space, she could breathe again. *But that would be short lived,* she thought, as she dropped her purse and sunglasses onto her desk. Because he wasn't going anywhere today.

She should just talk to him and get it over with. He could say whatever he needed to, then she could move on. Or at least get some closure. Then she could move on from this weird limbo she found herself in. He might have made it clear he wanted nothing to do with her, but she'd been in a rut since coming back to Orange Beach. Yeah, the salon was amazing, but her personal life? Non-existent. And she didn't want to find anyone else either. He'd completely screwed with her head.

As she started to take a sip from her drink, a grin spread across her face as her gaze landed on the big yellow sun costume tucked behind her desk. It was one of those costumes with arm holes that slid right over your head. The first week she'd opened she'd had one of her packmates—much to their horror—wear it a few times while standing out by the main road of the little shopping center holding a sign advertising the new salon. As cheesy as the advertising tactic was, it worked. And even if it wasn't something she wanted to use all the time—she was already so busy that walk-ins would just end up having to make future appointments, she really wanted to see Andrew wearing it. After what he'd done to her, he deserved to be punished.

Feeling only a little mean, she grabbed the costume and sign and headed out to the front.

* * *

"So, what did he do to warrant this punishment?" Erica asked quietly as she joined Charlie by the front window to watch Andrew do his thing.

Wearing that ridiculous smiley face sun over his clothes, he was spinning the advertising sign and acting as if he truly enjoyed his job. It was utterly ridiculous. Especially since he was mouth-wateringly sexy. Tall, good-looking, muscular, and doing the stupid job with a sexy-as-sin smile, he'd been pulling in a ton of customers all morning.

She'd extended her hours by one hour every day for the next three weeks so she wouldn't have to turn anyone away. "Is being male a good enough answer?" she muttered.

Erica laughed. "Usually. Show mercy on the guy. He did bring us all those donuts."

"Which you've all devoured."

Erica lifted an eyebrow. "What do you mean, *us*? I saw you eat a few yourself."

Charlie lifted a shoulder, grinning. "Who's going to turn down free donuts? Listen, I'm going to take my lunch now. You good to cover the phones while I'm gone?"

"Of course. Take the sexy wolf with you too. He deserves it."

Charlie nearly snarled at her friend for calling Andrew sexy. Which was ridiculous. Because he was just that. He wasn't hers though. She had no claim to him and she was trying very hard to convince her wolf of that. But her wolf could get possessive and irrational. At least where he was concerned because it had never happened before. Whatever Erica saw in Charlie's eyes made her grin.

She glanced over her shoulder, then turned back to Charlie. "When you extended your stay with the O'Shea pack... it was because of him, wasn't it?" she murmured so low Charlie barely heard her. At least her other packmates wouldn't overhear.

There was no reason to deny it. Erica would scent if she lied anyway. "Yeah."

Erica wrapped an arm around her shoulders and squeezed once. "I'm here if you want to talk." Erica might be younger, but she had a level head and was always the voice of reason.

"Thanks." She'd resisted talking about what had happened, but maybe she needed to get it out and let her pack take care of her. Ugh. Her wolf didn't know what she wanted. "I'm going to snag Andrew and take him to lunch." And just maybe she'd get some freaking closure. She'd used to think that was a stupid, made-up, human term, but now she completely understood.

"Ooh, you should have Andrew for lunch," one of the stylists said without looking up from the woman's hair she was working on.

Everyone in the salon giggled, but Charlie had to force herself not to release her claws. Gah. She hated this possessiveness, especially since she had no claim on him. Not anymore. Shaking those thoughts off, she just smiled good-naturedly and headed to her office to get her purse.

* * *

Andrew scented Charlie before he heard her. Turning to face her, sign in hand, all the muscles in his body tightened at the sight of her. He'd seen her this morning before she'd sent him out there, but it didn't matter.

Wearing a little dress that clung to her full hips and breasts, it fit her like a second skin, only reminding him that if he hadn't been a dumbass, he'd have the right to peel the dress from her and kiss every inch of her. He'd have the right to call her his, to let every other male know she was taken.

"You can take the sun off," she said. "I'm headed to lunch if you want to join me."

More than surprised by her show of civility, he nodded. He tugged the sun costume off and tucked it, along with the sign, under his arm. Pulling his keys from his pants pocket, he pressed the key fob. "I'll drive." He needed to be in control of something right now.

"Ah… okay." She nodded once and headed to his SUV with him. "I can drop the sign and sun off in the shop before we leave."

"Nah." He tossed it into the backseat before opening her door for her. He was thinking of burning the stupid thing.

She watched him tentatively for a moment before getting inside. As she slid past him, her wild scent made him want to groan and run his nose along her jaw and neck, nuzzle that sweet spot behind her ear. And now his vehicle would smell like her. He could drown in her scent. Without pause, he took the seatbelt and leaned across her, strapping her in.

She sucked in a breath and he froze, watching her for a long moment with only inches separating them. Her dark eyes dilated, her breath coming in shallow drags. It took all his self-control not to drop his gaze to her mouth—not to claim her mouth. He didn't have the right, however.

Using resolve he was surprised he possessed, he moved back, shutting the door behind him. He had to keep his head on straight, not push her too fast. If she forgave him at all, it was going to take time. He understood that.

Once in the driver's seat, he said, "Where to?"

"There's a pizza place a couple miles away. You'll like it," she murmured. "They've got a pizza called the New Yorker that you'll love. It's got three types of meat and jalapeños on it." Half-smiling, she let out a mock shudder because she hated jalapeños.

He wasn't sure how to take her friendliness, but it had to be a good sign. "Nice. Is it owned by your pack?"

"No. I figured maybe you wanted to talk without any eavesdropping shifters?"

Finding the words to tell her why he'd promised to come to her opening, then just not shown up—and stopped calling her would be hard enough without an audience. He wasn't looking forward to this. But it was time to man up. The courting was a good start, but he had to be honest with her. Lay himself bare. "Yeah, I do."

CHAPTER SIX

Andrew waited until their server had left the table. The college-aged kid had taken their order and already brought drinks so he and Charlie had time to talk. Alone. He rolled his shoulders once as he met Charlie's gaze.

There wasn't any anger there, just curiosity. Apparently she'd decided to be civil to him since she'd asked him to lunch and she wasn't snapping at him. Which somehow made this harder.

"I'm sorry, for everything," he finally said. "For breaking my word and not coming to your salon opening. For bailing on *us* more than anything. For not returning your calls. Overall, for acting like a complete and utter shit. It's not me and more than that, you didn't deserve it."

She blinked once and pushed out a breath. "Well... I didn't expect that."

He rubbed a hand over the back of his neck. "Sorry is inadequate, but I truly am."

"Is the reason you came down here to apologize?"

"That. And to ask for a second chance." He wasn't holding anything back. "Which I know I don't deserve."

She jolted a little, as if surprised by his admission. "Why?"

He didn't think she was asking why he wanted a second chance, but why he'd gone MIA. He rubbed the back of his neck again. He hated talking about this, hated everything about it. It made him feel vulnerable, exposed. As second-in-command, that wasn't an option. But he wasn't her second, he just wanted to be hers. "My mom died when I was young. Killed by a feral shifter… My dad mated again when I was twelve. Cora was an okay stepmom. Ridiculously strict, a control freak, but not abusive or anything. But the way she treated—treats—my dad… I never wanted that for myself. Swore I'd never let that happen to me."

Charlie frowned, but didn't interrupt.

"He does anything she wants, jumps when she says so. Her happiness is all that matters to him, above his own. They do whatever she wants, when she wants, whether it's where to go on vacation or what restaurant to eat at. She picked out the house they live in, tells him how to live his life, basically. She picks out his fucking clothes for him." He gritted his teeth, getting annoyed as he thought about it. "It's revolting to my wolf. I can't stand to see it."

She raised her eyebrows. "Okay. Was he like that with your mom?"

"I honestly don't remember. My memories of her are hazy but of a woman who doted on me. I don't know if she was the same way with him."

"You never asked him?"

"No. We argued about his current relationship when I was about eighteen. He told me it was normal, that sometimes you had to make sacrifices to make a mating work. But I know it's not normal. There's no compromise for them. It's all her way." He'd wanted to talk to his dad about his mother, to know if it had always been like this for his dad. He'd thought about it so many times. But he didn't have the best relationship with his father, barely saw him once a year anymore. After their argument, things had never been the same.

Yeah, he blamed it on being second-in-command and all the duties that entailed, but it was bullshit. The most alpha part of him had hated seeing his father, also an alpha, so cowed in every single thing. Being alpha didn't mean being in charge all the time. It was more of a physical strength thing. Often the emotional played into it for wolves too, but he couldn't deal with his dad's relationship, what the male had become because of his mate. This sad male who didn't even seem to recognize his own needs anymore.

"So… I'm glad you're telling me this, but what does this have to do with you and me?"

"When I met you I was hit hard by lust. Then it turned into something more. My wolf accepted you on a completely primal level and I found myself wanting to do anything to make you happy."

"Yeah, I felt the same way," she said quietly.

He paused once, then continued. "As I was getting ready to go to your salon opening, all I could think about was how long distance wasn't going to work for us. For me. Because I wanted to wake up to you every morning. I knew that as soon as I got down here, made that trip, it would be over for me. I could see myself following in my father's footsteps, giving up everything for a female. For you. And it freaked me the fuck out. Giving up everything I'd worked so hard for."

She leaned back in her seat, taking in his words and staying silent as the server dropped their food off. He didn't touch his pizza and she didn't make a move for her calzone.

"I don't know what to say," she finally said. "Other than I'm pretty pissed off." Even though she didn't raise her voice, and no one else around them would be able to overhear, he could scent her anger. It was tart and potent, filling the air so that if any shifter had been in the restaurant, they would be able to sense her agitation. "Did I ever tell you what to do or order you around?"

"No."

"Did I demand you come to Orange Beach?"

"No."

"Mates or intended mates or hell, just two people regardless of species who are in a relationship are supposed to want to make the other happy. Not to the point of losing who you are, but that's freaking normal."

"I know." He'd let his fear take over.

"You hurt me. I was so excited about you coming down here, about introducing you to my packmates. Then I got worried and I'm sure you know by now I called Alyssa. When she told me that you were fine, it was like..." Sighing, she shook her head, but she didn't have to finish.

Because he could imagine. If she'd done the same thing to him, he'd have gone crazy. Hell, he *had* been going crazy the past six weeks. "Charlie, if I could change what I've done, I would. I am sorry. I know you're not a control freak. I know you're nothing like my stepmother. I... screwed up."

Lifting her napkin from her lap, she set it on the table next to her plate. "I can sense that you're telling the truth, but it doesn't change anything. You hurt me. And you didn't even bother to talk to me about any of this. To tell me how you were feeling. To tell me about your history. You just decided to walk away. And..." Shaking her head, she stood. "I'm not storming off, but I don't want to be around you right now. It's only a couple miles back to the salon and I need some fresh air and space from you. If you really don't want to hurt me, then ask Max to transfer you somewhere else while you're in Orange Beach." She turned and left him sitting there.

Panic slammed through him, every instinct in his wolf telling him to go after her, to make this right, but he knew if he did that, he'd screw things up even worse. His wolf clawed at the surface, wanting out. He needed to shift and run, expend the rage he had— at himself. He'd been so worried about turning into his father and instead he'd pushed away the she-wolf who'd captured his heart. A female who was giving and kind.

Looking down at his food, he pushed the plate away. His stomach was balled too tight and the thought of food now was too much. He pulled out a couple bills, more than enough to pay for their food and leave a nice tip, and tossed them onto the table.

He would give Charlie the space she'd asked for, but he was still going to make sure she made it back to the salon okay.

Even if she never forgave him, he knew his wolf wouldn't settle for another female. He felt it bone deep. And he wasn't going to walk away from her without a fight. He'd apologized and told her the truth. Now it was time to make things right.

As he slid into his SUV, he pulled out his cell.

"Hey, everything okay?" Reece, his alpha asked, by way of greeting.

No. Because Andrew wouldn't be calling now just to talk. Not while Reece was at the alpha meetings. "Yeah, but we need to talk."

CHAPTER SEVEN

Charlie tossed back another shot, ignoring everyone and everything around her. Someone in the pack had decided to throw a party/BBQ at their private pool tonight. No special reason for it, because wolves didn't need one to have a good time.

The scent of barbequing chicken and sausage filled the air along with coconut oil and sunscreen. The sun had set an hour ago but some of her packmates had been at the pool all day. Fake tiki torches were posted around the four corners of the party zone and there was a game of volleyball going on in the pool. Someone had even created a makeshift dance floor. Normally the laughter of her packmates—and seeing some of the older ones trying to dance—made her feel good, soothed the wolf inside her.

Now… She took another shot.

"You okay?" Max slid onto the stool next to her, moving with the grace of the predator he was.

"Yep." She poured herself another shot—she'd brought her own bottle of tequila. It was definitely one of those nights.

"You sure about that?"

"Yep."

"Never seen you drunk before."

"Not drunk now." Shifters had ridiculously high metabolisms. All that shifting and running used a lot of energy. Which was good. Because if she'd been human, she'd have passed out on the bar by now.

"You're buzzed."

"True enough." She glanced at him. "You policing drinking now?"

He snorted and grinned. "Nah. I think we'd have a revolt in the pack. I'm just checking on one of my favorite packmates."

"Lauren send you over here?" Charlie glanced over her shoulder and saw Lauren stretched out on a lounge chair next to Sybil and Ella. They were all in their bathing suits, talking and laughing. Lauren had asked Charlie to join them, but she hadn't wanted to be a downer. So she was sitting here and drinking by herself. Freaking classy.

"Nope. Though I know my mate is worried about you. What's going on?"

"Nothing."

"Oh, okay. Well, if it's nothing." He rolled his eyes. "Come on. You're sitting here snarling at anyone who tries to sit next to you and you're drinking tequila." He lifted the bottle, which was over half-empty.

Stupid shifter genes. She couldn't even get properly drunk.

"I got an interesting call today," Max said when she didn't respond.

She loved Max; he was the go-to guy for wisdom most of the time. Especially if their alpha wasn't available. It was why he was such a kick ass second-in-command. But right now, she didn't want to open up about her drama with all her packmates around. They might not be intentionally eavesdropping, but it still happened occasionally. "Yeah?"

"From one of our visiting wolves."

She shoved her shot glass and mostly empty tequila bottle away from her. "I'm sure you did. If you want him to stay at the salon it's fine, I'll deal with it."

Max tilted his head slightly at her. "That's not—"

"I appreciate your concern. Seriously. But I really, really don't want to talk about him. Or anything." Because once she started, she was likely to get worked up and even more annoyed. Then everyone would be in her business. She grabbed Davis's arm as he passed her. "Push me around on the dance floor?" she asked him, feeling a tiny buzz now that she was on her feet.

Laughing, he nodded and set his beer bottle down on the bar next to Max. Older than her by about twenty or maybe thirty years, Davis was just as calm and steady as Max was. One of the most solid members of the pack. He mostly worked security at one of the hotels, restaurants or bars the pack owned because of his strength and status within the hierarchy. She'd heard he might even be promoted soon. Not that she cared about that.

She just wanted to dance for a bit, then go home. Coming out tonight had been a mistake but she was going to at least attempt to have fun.

"What's with the scent?" Davis asked as they moved onto the makeshift dance floor a few feet from the deep end of the pool—how was that a good idea?

"Eh." She started moving with the beat of the music, a light island mix that lifted her mood a little.

He laughed again. "All right, but I'm pretty sure I know what it is."

She doubted it, but let Davis take her hand and spin her once. Dancing was almost always guaranteed to make her feel good, but she'd never had a broken heart before Andrew.

She didn't care if they'd only spent a few weeks together, she'd fallen head over heels for Andrew. Something that had never happened to her before.

Even when she'd been in college she'd never done relationships lightly. She didn't do *anything* that way. When she committed she was loyal, all in.

So it burned that Andrew had just dumped all his baggage on her, assuming that what? That she'd start ordering him around, demand he move to Orange Beach? God, the male was obtuse.

When Davis abruptly pulled her close, her gaze jerked up to his. Before she could ask him what he was doing, he leaned down and nuzzled her neck.

Frozen for a moment, she pressed her hands against his shoulders. "What the hell was that?" Davis had never shown an ounce of interest in her—and vice versa. And nuzzling her neck was incredibly intimate, especially for a wolf. "You don't get that privilege," she snapped.

"You'll thank me later," he murmured, so low she barely heard him. "Your male has been watching you all night but he's been too much of a coward to make a move."

Wait, what? Andrew was here? She hadn't even scented him—which proved how screwed up her emotions were. She didn't have a chance to respond because a millisecond later, a blur of motion flew past her as Andrew tackled Davis, slamming his fist into her packmates' stomach.

"Andrew!" She took a step toward them, but immediately stopped herself. Getting in the middle of two males fighting was monumentally stupid. Especially two trained shifters.

Before she could decide what to do Max let out a loud, angry howl that had everyone stilling. The music dimmed, though didn't shut off completely.

She could see it pained Andrew to do so, but he shoved up from where he had Davis pinned on the ground and turned to face her as Max approached all of them. Andrew kept his blue gaze on hers as Max let out an annoyed growl. There was a wealth of emotions in Andrew's eyes, way too many to sift through.

"Davis, go home. And quit being such a troublemaker," Max muttered as he looked between Charlie and Andrew. "You two, my place now."

She had no choice but to follow the male and much to her annoyance, Andrew crowded all her personal space as they left the party. Okay, maybe she liked it. He kept his shoulder and arm against hers as the three of them rode in the elevator to the penthouse suite. Everyone was silent, making it even more awkward. He couldn't hide his wildly possessive and aggressive scent, however. It was wreaking havoc with her own emotions, knowing that he'd attacked Davis because of her. She wanted to tell Andrew that she hadn't been expecting Davis to do that and definitely hadn't allowed it, but they weren't together. She owed him nothing.

Still… her wolf felt almost guilty. Which simply annoyed her even more.

Inside the penthouse, Max finally stopped when they got to his living room. "Both of you, sit." He pointed to a long, white tufted couch that Lauren had no doubt picked out.

Even though Charlie wanted to pace, she followed orders and sat on one end of the couch. Andrew sat in the middle. Not right up next to her, but not on the other end. His dark scent was making her crazy.

"So," Max said, looking at Andrew, his wolf in his eyes. "You thought it was smart to attack one of my wolves during this trade? With Grant gone, I'm in charge, which you very well know."

Charlie stood up before Andrew could respond. Even if it wasn't her fault and she was still angry at him, she didn't want him to get in trouble for something Davis had apparently done intentionally to rile him up. She also didn't want to narc on her packmate.

"It wasn't Andrew's fault. I… was annoyed with him and baited him. I'll take whatever punishment you dole out," she hurriedly continued. Her scents were out of control now from drinking too much and from the wild emotions Andrew evoked inside her. Max might not be able to scent her lie because she couldn't even scent the acidic smell normally associated with a lie.

Max tilted his head slightly as he watched her.

"Double my punishment!" she blurted, hoping he'd just get this over with.

"No. That's ridiculous," Andrew snapped, standing. "I'm at fault here. I'll take all the punishment, whatever it is. You did nothing wrong. I attacked another male and deserve the punishment."

Max let his head roll back and let out a frustrated groan. "You all drive me insane." When he looked back at them, there was no anger in his expression or scent. "I don't know what's going on with you two and I've got enough on my plate now that I don't actually care. So, you'll be working patrol together the next couple days. You'll learn to get along and show the pack that a Kincaid member and an O'Shea member can be civil with each other. You put me in a rough spot by attacking Davis at the party. You both have to be punished, especially if you're admitting to baiting him?"

Charlie simply nodded because saying yes aloud would probably give her away. She hated patrols but knew their punishment could be a lot worse. Of course spending time with Andrew sucked, but she could deal with a couple more days. The trades couldn't take forever, right? Ugh.

"Does this mean no salon appointments?" she asked Max.

"Yes. Pass off your clients for the next two days. Patrols only."

She gritted her teeth, but nodded.

"You can go now," he said to her before turning back to Andrew. "You, stay."

Charlie didn't look directly at Andrew, but saw him watching her out of the corner of her eye as she walked past him. The heat of his gaze was scorching, as if he'd reached out and physically caressed her. Yeah, it was better that she didn't look at him. She might be pissed at him, but she still wanted the male. With an annoying intensity she couldn't begin to deny.

* * *

"Am I going to have a problem with you?" Max asked Andrew the moment Charlie was out of the condo.

Andrew wanted to go after her and ask her what the hell was going on with her and that male. And why she'd lied for Andrew. Her scents had been too jumbled but he was pretty certain she'd been lying about baiting him. Even if she had baited him, he deserved it.

"I've never lost control before. Not even as a pup." He rolled his shoulders once and walked to the window. He needed to stretch his legs, to run free. Anything to get out of his human form. His wolf might be wilder, but his animal had more clarity sometimes. Now was one of those times.

"Females can make males do stupid things." Max wasn't flat out asking anything and he didn't need to.

"True. But I take responsibility for what I did. None of what happened was on her." He'd seen that male lean down and rub his nose along Charlie's neck and Andrew had lost his mind. He didn't even remember moving. The only thing he did know was that he'd had to restrain himself from unleashing his claws, from shifting. The urge had been overwhelming, but he hadn't been so far gone that he'd lost that much control.

"Good response. Unfortunately she's taking responsibility, so she has to be part of the punishment."

Andrew understood completely. As second-in-command for the O'Shea pack he couldn't ever appear to show favoritism. It was another reason he'd never slept with anyone in his pack. Not before Charlie and definitely not since her. No female could hold a candle to her anyway. And his wolf wouldn't settle for anyone else, regardless. She was it for him. If she'd ever have him.

"What are your patrols like?" he asked, not wanting to talk more about Charlie.

"Likely similar to yours. Everyone works in shifts but the main focus is at night." He didn't have to say why. That was when vampires were out.

"When's the last time you had a vampire problem?"

"Couple months ago. Sometimes we get rogues in our territory. I don't know if you've met Rex yet?"

The name sounded familiar but Andrew couldn't place it. Charlie had told him about a lot of her packmates. "No."

"He's a vampire. Mated to one of our maternal she-wolves."

Andrew nodded, remembering now. "Okay."

"He'll be with his mate at her bakery tomorrow night, so ask Charlie to introduce you. Other than Rex, there shouldn't be any vamps in the area. You'll be teamed up with Charlie the whole time anyway. I'll let her know what areas I want patrolled and she'll tell you tomorrow."

"Okay. And I do apologize for earlier." He was here as part of a trade, something that was important to all of them. And he'd let himself get out of control.

"Davis was asking for it. My alpha doesn't have to mention it to your alpha."

"No, he should. I'll tell Reece myself anyway." He was always honest with his alpha. It was a vow he'd made when he'd agreed to take on the role of second.

Max nodded once, his expression approving, and Andrew was under the impression he'd passed some sort of test. "Go get some rest. Take the day to yourself tomorrow. Your patrol won't start until after sunset."

"Okay." Letting himself out, he followed Charlie's scent down to their floor.

Instead of moving past her door, like he knew he should, he stayed there for a long moment, inhaling deeply. Lust punched through him at her wild blueberries and peaches scent, his inner wolf clawing at him, not understanding why he couldn't be with her. Touch her, kiss her, bring her to orgasm.

It had been like that since she'd been gone, his dual natures at odds with each other as he tried to convince himself that staying away was the smart thing to do. In reality, it was insanity, trying to fight biology. His wolf had been edgier and edgier the more time that passed. Now he was on a razor's edge, barely in control of himself.

Pushing back from her door, he made his way to his condo. Tomorrow it would just be the two of them. He'd gotten a gift for her today and had planned to see if he could talk to her alone tonight to give it to her. Then he'd seen that male all over Charlie… no. He needed to stop thinking about that.

Otherwise his wolf was likely to do something beyond stupid and hunt that male down. Which would do no one any favors. It was only likely to get Andrew kicked out of the territory at best. And it definitely wouldn't win him any points with Charlie.

Still, he wondered if she'd been with that male or was planning to hook up with him. His claws extended. He was unable to stop the primal reaction at the thought of another male touching his female.

Nope. Time to put all those thoughts on lockdown. Tomorrow night at least, Charlie would be his for a few hours of uninterrupted time. He'd already told her the truth. Now he had to get her to forgive him and win her back for good.

CHAPTER EIGHT

Charlie took a deep breath and opened her front door—and came face-to-face with sexy-as-sin Andrew. She'd scented him, but thought it was just because he was on this floor. "Hey." Why did she sound all breathy? There would be no breathiness, no sexiness. Nada. Tonight they were going to be two professionals on patrol acting like civilized wolves.

Her inner wolf nearly snorted. Yeah right, that was why she'd worn her tight cargo pants and skin tight matching tank top. Liar, liar, sexy pants on fire.

He swept his gaze over her so quickly she might have missed it, but there was no ignoring the glint of hunger in his pale eyes when their gazes clashed again. God, this male was determined to drive her insane simply with his presence. And oh, what a presence it was. Tall, dark, sexy, he was dressed similarly to her with dark cargo pants and a T-shirt that did nothing to hide those sculpted abs and muscles. His broad shoulders stretched against the fabric of the shirt, begging for her to tear it off.

"Did you bait me last night?" he asked by way of greeting.

She blinked once, taken off guard by the question. "What?"

"It's a yes or no answer."

She pursed her lips and stepped outside fully, pulling the door shut behind her. "You ready for tonight? I've got our patrol area mapped out but we can stop by Margery's bakery first. Max said something about wanting you to meet Margery's mate, Rex, so you know who the only vampire living in our territory is."

"I'm going to take your deflection as a no. Why'd you try to take the blame for me when I acted like a pup and attacked that asshole?" He had no choice but to fall in step with her as she started heading down the hallway.

"Who said I did?"

"You did with your non-answer."

Charlie was trying to deflect because she didn't want him to scent her lie. Last night emotions had been too high. It had been the only way she'd covered up the acidic scent. Of course now he wanted to push. Gah. Well, there was no point in lying. "Fine. No, I didn't bait you. Davis—"

Andrew's sharp growl abruptly cut her off as they reached the top of the stairs.

She froze, staring at him. "What's that for?"

"I don't like you saying his name. Or any male's name for that matter."

That was completely insane. But oh how her wolf liked this crazy possessive side of him. He'd been like that back in South Carolina too, not liking it when any of his pack's males—even the happily mated ones—got too close to her. Or talked to her too much.

"Okay, then the male who shall not be named might have taken it upon himself to act like an utter jackass. Pretty sure he wanted to bait you for some inane reason only males understand. But I wasn't going to narc him out to Max."

Her words seemed to soothe Andrew a fraction as they started down the stairs. His scent, mixed with the salty ocean made her wolf ridiculously happy. Which made no sense. She wasn't happy about being stuck with him. Nope, not happy at all. Well, her wolf hadn't gotten the memo because she wanted to prance around and show off for him. Her wolf still wanted him to pay for his ghosting act, but man, she was horny too.

"You ever hooked up with him?"

She blinked again. "Not that it's your business, but no. And you don't get to ask that question again.

About anyone." She'd never actually been with anyone in the pack. No, thank you. That was like asking for drama. Wolves, even if they knew things were just casual, could get all territorial and cranky. Especially males.

"I've never been with anyone in my pack," he said matter-of-factly.

The info shouldn't please her, but it definitely did. "Me neither." Damn it, why did she tell him that?

He seemed to stand up taller at that. "I wish I could say I was sorry about last night, but I'm glad we're on patrol together."

She sniffed a little at that, but agreed. At least her wolf side did. "You want to drive?" she asked as they reached the bottom floor.

"Doesn't matter."

"Sure it won't offend your alpha sensibilities for me to take control?" She felt a little bitchy asking the question, but she was still dealing with his confession.

To her surprise, he grinned at her. Actually grinned. She couldn't figure out what the hell he was smiling about, either.

"I've been rethinking my jackassery—"

"Jackassery?"

"That's what Sybil calls it."

"Smart she-wolf," Charlie murmured.

"And I can think of a few ways I wouldn't mind you taking control." He dropped his voice a few octaves, making his already deep voice even more delicious.

Before she could attempt to cover her scent or control her reaction, hunger surged through her like a wildfire, electrifying all her nerve endings until everyone in a mile radius would be able to scent her need. Oh, hell. She clenched her thighs together as they reached his SUV, but it was pointless. Nothing could ease her ache but him. Since that wasn't happening, she'd just have to suffer. "You can't just say stuff like that anymore."

"Oh, I can say whatever I want. I plan to win you back," he said, leaning into her until she pressed her back against the passenger side door. His wild scent enveloped her as much as his huge body did. He placed his hands on either side of her head, caging her in, but not touching her.

He didn't need to. All she wanted to do was arch up into him, to rub her body all over his. Her only saving grace was that his scent was just as intense, wrapping around her and letting any supernaturals in the vicinity know that he was turned on. For her.

"One day at a time, and I've got all the time in the world."

"You'll be leaving soon," she whispered, barely able to find her voice.

"I've put in for a transfer."

Wait... what? She couldn't find her voice, could barely digest what he'd said as he opened the door for her and guided her into the passenger seat. She didn't even protest as he strapped her in. "You couldn't have put in for a transfer," she finally croaked out as he slid into the driver's seat.

"I did. And you'll have to tell me where I'm going," he said as he steered toward the main gates. "I'm not sure where the bakery is."

"But... you're second-in-command. That spot is already taken here." He couldn't have volunteered to give up all that. It went completely against his nature.

"Well, I'll adjust."

No. She'd been so angry at him. Now she simply felt panicked. This wasn't what she'd wanted. "Turn left... and Andrew, you can't just adjust. Second-in-command is part of who you are, and I didn't ask you to do this." No, this could never work. Hierarchies in packs were important to wolves and unlike him, it would be easier for her to transfer somewhere. Not because of her gender but because of who she was. Yeah, she'd miss her pack, but he'd miss an intrinsic part of himself if he left his. Eventually he'd become resentful. And even if he didn't, he would always feel like he was missing part of himself. That wasn't something she could live with. She cared for him too much.

"I know. But I'm serious about you. About us. I love—"

"No!" She didn't want to hear the words now. Her emotions were already tangled enough. She couldn't hear him tell her that he loved her. No, no, no.

"Even if I don't say them out loud, it doesn't change the truth of my feelings." There was no hesitation in his voice and the truth was in his scent. "I want to make it crystal fucking clear that you're it for me, Charlie. I screwed up before. Big time. I own it. And now I'm going to win you back. That means we need to live in the same city. I'm not being separated from you again. You're mine," he said, looking at her as they pulled up to a red light. Unabashed lust glittered in his eyes.

She wanted to hit something. "Damn it, Andrew! I'm so mad at you right now! I would have moved to South Carolina! In fact, I'd hoped you would ask me—until you disappeared from my life. But *this* isn't what I wanted." She absently motioned for him to take another turn. It was a good thing she could get to Margery's in her sleep because she could barely concentrate on anything right now.

He looked forward once again, not trying to mask the scent of his hunger for her. She pulled out her cell phone and texted Alyssa. No matter what happened, she couldn't let Andrew make this choice for her. Even if she was still holding on to some anger, this was a huge sacrifice. One he seemed to have no problem making. Which soothed all of her wolf's lingering annoyance.

Her fingers flew across the keypad at lightning speed. *Don't let Andrew transfer from the pack. He's lost his freaking mind. I know you're busy but call me when you get a break.*

It would have to do for now. When she talked to Alyssa, she'd make sure to straighten things out. Even as she had the thought, the pleasure she felt that he was willing to move here for her, to show what she meant to him… it changed everything. She wasn't okay with how everything had gone down, but she wasn't letting him do this. No way.

* * *

Andrew watched as Charlie talked with Margery behind the display case of pastries and cakes. She was more relaxed than he'd seen her with anyone and it was clear to see why. Margery was definitely one of the maternal wolves of the pack. Someone everyone likely went to for advice. And the female was mated to a very decent vampire, it seemed.

"If you want some help with your patrols tonight, let me know," Rex said, pulling Andrew's attention away from watching Charlie. "I know Charlie is familiar with the area, but she's not normally on patrol."

Yeah, and it was his fault that she hadn't been able to work at her salon today. He kept the sentiment to himself, however. "Isn't it your night off?" Charlie had said something about the vampire helping out with security and anything else their alpha wanted.

Rex shrugged. "Yeah, but Margery's working, so... if you need the help, I like to stay busy."

"I'll let you know." He wouldn't be calling anyone though. Not when he had a chance to have Charlie all to himself. He'd already laid the gauntlet down, let her know exactly what his intentions were. He might have screwed up before, but all he could do was move forward now. With her in his life. Wherever they lived didn't matter. If he had to take on a different role in this pack, so what? It was worth it if he had her as his mate.

Rex snorted. "I won't expect a call then."

Andrew half-smiled and lifted a shoulder. "I'm not sharing my time with her."

"I understand," Rex said, his own gaze straying to Margery, a tall, slender woman with dark hair and eyes.

She was pretty, but no one compared to the compact beauty right next to her. As if she sensed his thoughts, or felt his gaze on her, Charlie turned toward him. Her eyes went heavy-lidded and for just a moment, her wolf peered back at him.

His own wolf rose in response to all that heat and need. When Rex nudged him, he realized the vampire must have said his name more than once. Blinking, Andrew turned to look at the male. "What?"

"You two need to get out of here and find some privacy." There was no admonishment in the vampire's words, but Andrew knew why Rex was telling him that.

He and Charlie were throwing off all sorts of hormones—which could affect any supernaturals or even humans, though the latter wouldn't realize it. It wasn't even a bad thing, but he needed to get himself under control.

If only it were that easy. He knew he had an uphill battle with her—and winning her trust back. But he was up to the job.

CHAPTER NINE

"It's quiet out here," Andrew said, mainly just to break the silence as he pulled into a driveway at the end of a long, quiet road. Since leaving Margery's bakery Charlie had been quiet. He wasn't sure if it was because she was angry at him, because her scents were wild and filled with lust.

Which was just driving his wolf insane. It didn't understand why they weren't naked right now.

"Yeah, all these homes are vacation rentals. Short term stuff. The pack uses them for income, but Grant wanted to have them remodeled and up-graded. Said it would be easier to have them all done at once instead of spread out."

"Makes sense." Then they wouldn't have any an-noyed renters dealing with construction. The gentle lapping of the ocean waves filled the air as he opened his door. The group of two-story homes were mostly lit up. A huge tile-saw sat in the current driveway. The builders should have put that back in the garage, though this far out it was unlikely anyone would steal it. Still, it was stupid. "Are your wolves doing the remodels?"

She snorted as she rounded the front of the SUV to meet him. "No. Not this one anyway. With the new hotel and Grant expanding some of our territory, it was easier to hire humans for the job." She frowned at the tile-saw. "Stupid to leave this out."

Andrew nodded once in agreement as he visually scanned the area. He couldn't scent anything off, but that didn't mean anything. There were a lot of residual scents, mostly of humans, lingering in the air. He also scented old cigarettes and a few animals nearby at the beach. "How do you normally do this?" he asked, wanting her to take lead.

This was her pack's territory after all.

She looked as if she might say something—probably a smartass comment, if her expression was any indication—then cleared her throat. "I'm not big on patrols. Kinda hate them, actually. I used to pick up shifts for packmates at the bar so I wouldn't have to do patrols. So I'll let you run the show if you'd like."

"You hate patrols?" She'd never told him.

She nodded, her lips kicking up at the corners. "Yes. So boring."

That wasn't always the case, not for him anyway, but he was glad her patrols weren't exciting. If they were, it meant she was fighting someone or having to police shifters or vampires stupid enough to invade a wolf pack's territory. The thought of her in any sort of danger made him crazy.

"And I like interacting with people."

"What about humans?" he asked, motioning that they should head around the house. All the homes were on a long strip of beach front property. It would be easy enough to patrol the beach, then loop back around and check out each individual front and backyard. Their sense of smell was good enough that they wouldn't have to enter each place unless they seemed occupied.

"Yeah, humans too. I like all the humans who come into the salon. Or most of them anyway. They've always got funny stories and it's better than gossiping about pack stuff."

He laughed. "Yeah, our pack is the same way." Wolves were so nosy it was almost impossible to have privacy. Though he was pretty certain she hadn't told anyone about them. He wondered why. "Can I ask you something?"

"Yeah." She fell in step with him as they reached the private walkway behind the current house.

The crash of the waves was louder here and he had a perfect visual of the ocean. With a near full moon it would be easy to see if anyone was along this stretch of beach. It wasn't private, but these homes were far enough down from all the hotels and bars it was unlikely that there would be joggers. Locals maybe, but that was it.

"Most of your pack—before last night—didn't seem to know about us."

"That's not a question."

"Okay, why didn't you tell them about us?"

"I'd planned to introduce you to everyone at the salon opening. I'd wanted to keep what we had to myself for a little bit. I…I'd never been in love before, so I liked having it private. They all know about us now. Or at least they're speculating."

He pretty much filtered out everything after 'love'. "Did you just say—"

They both froze at a faint, distinctive scent on the air.

"Is that a vampire?" Charlie murmured as they stepped onto the last stair before reaching the sandy beach.

He nodded and they both grew silent. He motioned that they move back along the dock. Once they reached midpoint, he used hand signals that they should jump over the edge behind a sand dune.

Charlie moved with him, her movements economical and graceful. Her boots were silent as she landed in the sand.

"Would you head back to the SUV and wait for me?" he murmured low enough that his voice wouldn't carry. He wasn't surprised when she just glared. Okay, he wouldn't leave her behind, he couldn't expect her to do it to him. But he wanted her safe. Always. Well, he was just going to have to get over his alpha possessiveness—for right now— and they would work as a team. "Okay, I'll have your back no matter what."

"I know." The absolute faith in those two words humbled him.

He might have screwed up before, but he wouldn't let her down now. No way in hell.

Inhaling deeply, he scented at least two distinctive supernatural scents. Vampires, he was almost certain by the cooler scent. It was like a light vanilla. Barely a hint on the air but he knew what direction it was coming from. Pointing to the west, he was glad when Charlie nodded.

She scented it in the same direction as him.

Staying in front of her, he moved through the foliage and underbrush along the sand dune until he reached another private dock of the house next door. The scent was stronger now.

So were moans. Not... pleasure either. He scented blood. And a human.

So did Charlie if the angry wolf that appeared in her eyes was any indication. He preferred to fight in wolf form, but until he knew what was going on, he'd remain human. They both climbed over the ledge of the dock, hoisting up and over on silent feet before jumping over the other side. The sand muted their movements as they hurried across the other dune.

The moaning had stopped but the metallic scent of blood was stronger now. As they neared the next private dock he spotted dark figures up by the pool behind this particular house. He looked at Charlie and motioned for her to head around to the beach then come up from behind the figures. It was clear she understood and as soon as she took off, he used the shadows to move in on the predators in the Kincaid pack's territory.

The closer he got to the pool, he realized that two vampires, young for vampire standards if their scent was any indication, were feeding on a human woman. Each vamp had a wrist and the woman was preternaturally still.

He didn't scent any others nearby but if there were, he'd just have to attack and trust Charlie to watch his back. He had to help this woman. Grabbing the edge of the dock, he hoisted himself over. Either his scent or a noise alerted the vamps to his presence because they both raised their heads at the same time.

Twin pairs of amber eyes glowed back at him. They were about thirty feet away, on the patio, but with his supernatural vision he had a clear view of them. One male, one female, looked to be in their late twenties.

No need for subtlety now. Growling low in his throat, he let his canines and claws extend and raced at them.

The vamps hissed as they abandoned their victim, the female running away as the male faced off with him. But Andrew wasn't fooled. The female would try to come around and attack him from behind. Unless she was a complete coward and abandoning her partner. Vamps weren't often like shifters in the pack mentality.

The male vampire raced right at him, his eyes wild as he moved with a supernatural speed.

Andrew used his own speed and strength and dodged to the side as the vamp slashed out at him with sharp claws. Moving low, Andrew twisted and sliced out at the vamp's back.

The vampire shrieked as Andrew drew blood, opening up massive wounds along the male's back. It vaguely registered how thin the vampire was, how drawn and pale his face was as the male turned back to attack again.

But all Andrew cared about was ending this threat so he could take out the female. Before Charlie had to fight her. Normally he liked a longer fight, but he needed to get to Charlie now. He couldn't scent her because of all the blood and it was making him edgy. Moving lightning fast, he slammed his fist across the male's jaw. Sensation barely registered as the vamp flew back a few feet.

Using his supernatural speed, Andrew covered the distance between them and slashed out with his other hand, flaying the guy's chest open before attacking again. This time, he used his razor sharp claws and cut off the male's head in one, clean swoop.

Before the head could hit the concrete patio, it turned to ash along with the rest of the body.

Blood pumping, Andrew jumped through the still falling ash as he raced across the patio, skirting the pool and the too still human as he followed the scent of the escaped female vamp.

He needed to find her, kill her. And make sure Charlie was okay. More than anything—

Charlie stepped out from around the side of the house, wiping her hands on her dark pants. Ash covered her tank top but she was unharmed.

His heart rate increased when he scented blood. Her blood. He was in front of her in milliseconds. "You're hurt."

"I'm fine." She waved away his words. "Just a few scratches. Were there more than two?"

"No. But—"

"We've got to get the human to the nearest hospital. I can hear her breathing. Barely."

Hell. She was right. He wanted to inspect her, to make sure she was a hundred percent okay, but they had to do this. If this human was going to have a fighting chance, she was going to need more blood because there was no telling how much the vampires had taken. "Let's go." Without waiting he hurried over to the human and lifted her into his arms. "You'll have to direct me to the hospital."

"I will. I'm going to call Max on the way and have him send a team down here to scour for more vampires."

He nodded once but glanced at her as they hurried back the way they'd come. He still scented her blood. And he wasn't sure if it was a lot or if his wolf was just going crazy because the thought of Charlie injured in any way made him want to go feral.

As soon as they were alone he was checking every inch of her to make sure she was okay. It didn't matter that things weren't right between them yet, she was his to take care of.

CHAPTER TEN

"I'm fine." Charlie batted away Andrew's hand as he tried to bandage her rib. "Look, I'm almost healed." The female vampire had gotten in a few slashes before Charlie had taken her head off. Ugh. She'd killed a vampire in the past, but it wasn't something she enjoyed. She didn't feel guilty since the vamp had been trying to drink a human dry, but it was still something she could live without doing. As a wolf she liked to hunt, but violence like this was shocking to her senses.

He took a small step back from where she was perched on the edge of her kitchen counter and eyed her from head to toe. Unfortunately there was no heat in his clinical perusal. After dropping the human off at the local hospital—and calling Max to let him know, they'd come back to her condo.

Since she was sitting in a sports bra and boyshort panties, she should be getting some sexy vibes from him, but nope. He'd made her strip, then cleaned all traces of blood from her body. And there hadn't been much. Now she just had a rapidly healing cut on her rib and one on her upper thigh. And that one was...

"Look." She grabbed the hand towel from him and wiped her leg. "This one is already healed. I'm a freaking wolf, you know we heal faster than humans." But the male had gone ultra-protective. Which was, okay, pretty sweet.

Before he could respond, she heard her front door open and a handful of packmates entering. Of course they wouldn't knock, not when they knew she'd been injured. A few seconds later Max, Lauren and four other wolves streamed into her kitchen.

To her surprise, Andrew stood half in front of her. "Is everything okay with the human?" he demanded of Max.

Max didn't seem annoyed by Andrew's tone. He simply nodded. "Yep. She's going to make it and I've got a friend keeping an eye on the situation. We're not sure if she remembers what happened with the vampires or not. Seems as if she was taken from a local club. Might have been drugged beforehand."

"Good. Since that's not an issue, everyone can get the hell out," he snapped, moving to stand fully in front of her now. His scent was dark and wild and it was really turning her on.

Charlie heard a couple of the females gasp, but Max just sighed. "Everyone, out. Call me if you need me, Charlie," he said, before his footsteps followed the others.

When Andrew turned back to her, his expression was hard and just a little dangerous. "No one is taking care of you but me." The way he said it was as if he was expecting an argument.

"Okay."

"Wh... that's right it's okay. You're my female, Charlie."

Her nipples tightened at the heat in his voice. "Okay." She wasn't going to fight it or put him through the ringer. Maybe she should, but after fighting that vampire and losing blood she was exhausted. And tonight had just been a reminder how short life could be, even for supernaturals. Her kind might have a longer life span than humans, but there was no guarantee they would make it to old age. And the way she felt right now, she wanted the chance to make it to her old age, with Andrew by her side. She wanted him to claim her. Finally.

His eyes narrowed a fraction. "I'm full on claiming you. I want to move in with you, mate with you... marry you. I want it all. I love you, Charlie."

Her heart skipped a beat. This was what she'd wanted to hear, what her wolf needed to hear. He'd screwed up, yes, but he'd also apologized and was trying to make things right. After tonight, she didn't want to be separated from him anymore. "Okay, to all of the above. On one condition."

He tensed, all his muscles pulling taut as he stood before her looking good enough to eat. "What?"

"That you don't move here. I'll move with you."

"But your business—"

"I can move my business. There's not a spot for a new second here. And it's not likely to open up anytime soon. Hopefully never. The only thing I ask for, is that you're honest with me. That we communicate about our issues. No disappearing acts again. Because if there's ever a second time, I'll slice you to ribbons."

He covered the foot of distance between them and cupped her cheeks with his big palms. "I'd expect nothing less. And I won't be disappearing again. You're the best thing that ever happened to me. Since we've been apart... I've been miserable. Nothing is right without you. I love you, Charlie." It was the second time he'd said it in the last sixty seconds and it made warmth bloom inside her, flooding her entire system. He crushed his mouth to hers as he slid in between her legs, spreading them wider with his hips.

She wrapped her legs around him as she met his tongue stroke for stroke. Heat surged through her, pooling between her legs as he teased her tongue with his. She'd been fantasizing about him since the day they'd met. Even when they'd been apart, he'd still starred in her fantasies.

He rolled his hips, his thick erection rubbing against her covered mound. Unfortunately he was still fully dressed.

Reaching between their bodies, she grabbed the edge of his T-shirt and tugged it upward. When he leaned back to rip it off, his wolf was clear in his gaze, looking back at her. Both parts of him accepted all of her. It was the same for her too. She'd accepted his animal nature even before she'd known him on a deeper level.

"Here, or your room?" he rasped out.

"Doesn't matter." She didn't care where they did this as long as she finally got to feel him sinking deep inside her. Her inner walls clenched at the thought of him filling her.

He scooped her up so that she wrapped her legs around him again and headed straight for her bedroom. Even with her sports bra, there was a lot of skin on skin as she met his mouth again with her own.

His taste was intoxicating, making her lightheaded as they reached her bedroom. Soon enough, this wouldn't be her room anymore because she'd be living with him. The thought didn't scare her either. Moving with him, getting to fall asleep and wake up beside him was going to be an adventure. The best one she would ever have.

"Can't wait to taste you," he murmured against her mouth a second before she tumbled onto the bed, him right on top of her.

Moaning in agreement, she wanted to taste more of him too. "Clothes, off. Now." She was impressed she could get out three whole words. Her body was a live wire right now.

Instead of taking off his pants, as she'd hoped, he grasped the edge of her boyshort panties. "Take your bra off." The subtle command in his voice had her nipples tightening even more.

She did as he said, tossing it to the side as he tugged the rest of her clothing off. She shivered as he raked his scorching hot gaze over the length of her.

Going still, he crouched at the end of the bed, staring at her as if he could devour her—as if she was the most beautiful female he'd ever seen. She spread her thighs even wider, a thrill shooting through her when he growled low in his throat.

Oh yeah, she wanted him to lose control. She was on a ledge right now and wanted to fall over it with him.

Andrew drank in the sight of his female stretched out before him. Her soft skin seemed to glow under the moonlight streaming in from her wide open windows. The moon bathed her, highlighting all of her perfection.

It seemed as if he'd been waiting forever for her. He couldn't believe she was giving him a second chance so quickly, but he wasn't going to question it. No, he was going to show her that he deserved the chance.

That they deserved the happiness.

When she spread her legs wider for him, his brain short-circuited. "Charlotte," he murmured, loving the sound of her full name. His Charlie.

"Do something." The words were part plea, part demand and he loved all of it. He'd been so caught up in his bullshit that he hadn't realized how very sexy it could be for Charlie to make *some* demands of him.

"Tell me what you want."

Her cheeks flushed a sexy shade of red as she lifted her hips up. He wondered if she was even aware of the action or if it was just her body taking over. "Your mouth, my pussy. *Please.*"

Oh, fuck. That propelled him into action. His cock pulsed heavy, desperate to be inside her, but he was going to taste her come first. He'd tasted her before and he'd been craving her ever since their separation. She was his addiction.

After this, he wasn't going to be apart from her again. Not happening. His wolf still hadn't forgiven him, wasn't even sure this was real. If it was a dream, it was the best one he'd ever had.

Slowly, he leaned down between her legs, inhaling her sweet scent before he just barely ran his tongue up her slick, soft folds.

She speared her fingers into his hair, cupping his head as he began teasing her. She tasted like heaven. Like his.

Her moans filled the bedroom as he continued flicking his tongue along her folds until her fingers dug into his scalp, the bite of pain sending a shock of pleasure through him. He knew what she wanted.

Focusing on her clit, he used enough pressure to drive her crazy, but not quite push her over the edge. He was saving that for when he was inside her. He wanted to feel her inner walls pulsing around his cock, to feel her heat as she came around him.

He moaned against her just thinking about it. The scent of her lust was potent and sharp, wrapping around them and mixing with his own.

Sliding his hands up the smooth skin of her thighs, he forced himself to lift his head. She stared down at him, her chest rising and falling. "You're stopping?"

He shook his head and quickly shucked the rest of his clothes. When he settled between her legs, he leaned over her, caging her in with his arms and body so that inches separated them.

Her dark eyes flared brightly as she rolled her hips up to meet his. Her slick folds rubbed against the head of his cock.

He thought about asking her if she was sure, but he knew she was. When she reached around his body and grabbed his ass, he grinned, slanting his mouth over hers as he thrust inside her.

She dug her fingers into his backside as he slid all the way home. Her inner walls were tighter than he'd imagined, sending all thought out the window.

He reached between their bodies and began teasing her clit as she started moving her hips. They fell into a rhythm as he thrust inside her over and over until he knew she was close. Her inner walls started convulsing around him, faster and faster.

His balls pulled up tight at the sensation, at the feel of *her* around him. He needed her to come, was desperate for it as he buried his face against her neck.

When he felt the bite of her canines against his shoulder, his own canines pierced her soft skin. Pleasure punched out to all his nerve endings at the feel of her marking him. He liked that she was claiming him the same way he was her. They'd officially mate later, but this was everything to him. Her marking him like this would let everyone know they were together. And everyone would know she was his.

And when he felt her climax hit, the rush of heat around his cock as she let go, he did the same. His orgasm slammed through him like a battering ram as he came inside her, thrusting over and over until they were both spent.

Looking down at her, too many emotions assaulted him at once. But mainly, love.

"I don't think I said the words earlier, but I love you." Charlie raised a hand to his face, her palm cupping his cheek and beard.

"I know… Once we get back to South Carolina I want to officially mate." He wanted her locked down forever. This was a female he'd be crazy to let go. Once they were mated, they'd be linked for life. And every supernatural being would know she was off-limits. And vice versa for him.

"We don't have to wait that long." Her eyes were heavy-lidded as she looked up at him.

It took all of a second for her words to register. Just like that he was hard again. "You're sure?"

"Yep. You might have screwed up, but before all that, I knew what I wanted. When I'm in, I'm all in. I'm not walking away from this so if *you* have doubts—"

"Hell no." He growled again, something that seemed to be a perpetual problem around her. She made him all snarly and protective in a way he'd never imagined. He'd seen other mated males lose their mind over females but had never imagined it could happen to him.

Charlie had changed his entire world. And he didn't mind the loss of control around her.

Taking her face between his hands, he kissed her long and hard. It looked like they were in for a long night. Later, he'd let Max know they wouldn't be on any patrol tomorrow night. Or the night after. He wasn't letting Charlie leave his bed. Not for a week, at least.

Soon, he'd have her at his house—their house. And they could start their new life together.

One month later

Charlie finger-combed her damp hair as she stepped into their walk-in closet. Since moving to South Carolina with Andrew she'd discovered even more perks than the man himself. Like a closet that had more than enough room for all her clothes and shoes, with room left over.

"Charlie!" At the sound of Andrew's panicked voice she hurried out of the closet to find him racing into their room, slightly out of breath. He paused for a moment, his gaze sweeping over her naked body. Then he shook his head slightly. "Been calling you."

"I was in the shower." And she was pretty sure she'd left her phone downstairs. "What's going on?"

"Alyssa's having her baby. I just got the call."

Time to go then. Stepping back into the closet, Charlie grabbed the first summer dress she saw and pulled it over her head. Then she grabbed the nearest sandals. "Do you know how she's doing?" Charlie asked as she hurried after him.

"She's surprisingly fine. *She* called me."

"Where's Reece?"

"He was driving and apparently refused to do anything but drive. He didn't want to be focused on anything other than getting her to the doctor. Alyssa sounded a little exasperated with him."

Charlie just snorted as they hurried out the front door. That sounded about right. Their alpha had been beyond protective this last month, going so far as keeping everyone a few feet away from his mate when someone visited the alpha couple's house. And Andrew seemed to think that behavior was totally normal.

He tossed her the keys to his SUV as they reached the driveway. "You drive. I've got a ton of calls to make. Promised Alyssa I'd call her dad and her former packmates."

In seconds they were on the road, heading to the pack's doctor and the private shifter-only clinic they owned. Shifters were pregnant a full two, sometimes two and a half months shorter than humans, so Alyssa was right on time.

Charlie was silent as Andrew made a round of calls. Finally he set his phone down, sighing in relief. They'd be at the clinic in about five minutes.

"Her father's coming out today and he'll let his packmates know when it's okay to visit."

"Probably better that way." Alyssa's old pack lived only a few towns over, but Reece wouldn't want a bunch of people crowding him, his mate and their new baby. Andrew definitely had to be there because he was the second-in-command. Part of his duties included protecting the alpha's family at a time like this.

Not that anyone was worried about an attack, but the entire pack would go on lockdown and increase patrols until the baby was a month old. Probably longer, knowing Reece.

"You ready to deal with all the craziness that's about to follow?" she asked him, reaching out to take his hand with hers. He'd be basically taking over for Reece for a little while as the alpha adjusted to life as a new dad. Heck, he'd been doing more than normal since they'd moved back home.

She'd been worried about adjusting to such a big move, but he'd been her rock during the upheaval. Even while taking on extra duties for his pack, she'd never once felt neglected. And he'd surprised her with the funds to buy any property she wanted for her new salon. She hadn't wanted to take the money, but it had been so important to him that she got the perfect place so she'd agreed. She'd actually found the perfect place today, and had planned to ask Andrew to come with her to check it out, but that would definitely have to wait.

He linked his fingers through hers, squeezed tight. "I am since you're by my side."

She smiled, glancing at him as they came to a stoplight. Since she'd moved up here he'd been crazy busy. The couple weeks both he and Reece had been gone had sent the pack into a bit of stress. They were a young pack and needed constant leadership more than an older pack would have. She was impressed by how easily Andrew seemed to handle everything.

"You'll be happy to know I have a bag of snacks packed as well as a couple extra changes of clothes for us if we need it," she said. "I've got them stashed in the back of the SUV. And before you ask, I knew she was coming up on her due date and wanted to be prepared."

"Not sure how I got lucky enough to call you my own," he murmured.

"Right back at you." She looked at him again and sucked in a breath at the sight of the clear love in his pale gaze. Seeing it didn't get old and she didn't think it ever would. Moving from her old pack had been an adjustment, but she wouldn't give Andrew up for anything or anyone. Every day of their new life together was better than the last. Since settling in together she'd woken up every morning to a gift from him. Usually something small, like a little card telling her how much he loved her. Or flowers. But the best part, was waking up to fresh coffee. Her weakness. Well, other than Andrew.

"So when do you think you'll be ready to start a family of our own?" His tone was cautious.

She didn't have to think about the answer. "A couple years." They'd talked about kids in an abstract way and she knew he wanted them. Shifters usually did. She did too, but not right now.

He let out a sigh as they pulled into the parking lot of the clinic. "Same here. I'm still enjoying having you all to myself." Leaning over, he nuzzled her mating mark, sending a spiral of heat through her straight to her toes.

"Oh yeah," she murmured, leaning into his kiss as she put the SUV in park. "And you have the worst timing."

Groaning, he pulled back and unstrapped his seatbelt. "No kidding. As soon as this kid is born and we're back home, it's on."

"I like the sound of that." Of both having him all to herself and the word home. For the first time in her life, she understood that home wasn't a place. Home was wherever Andrew was. She was never letting him go.

Thank you for reading Falling For His Mate. I really hope you enjoyed it. If you don't want to miss any future releases, please feel free to join my newsletter. Find the signup link on my website: http://www.savannahstuartauthor.com

COMPLETE BOOKLIST

Miami Scorcher Series
Unleashed Temptation
Worth the Risk
Power Unleashed
Dangerous Craving
Desire Unleashed

Crescent Moon Series
Taming the Alpha
Claiming His Mate
Tempting His Mate
Saving His Mate
To Catch His Mate
Falling For His Mate

Futuristic Romance
Heated Mating
Claiming Her Warriors
Claimed by the Warrior

Contemporary Erotic Romance
Dangerous Deception
Everything to Lose
Adrianna's Cowboy
Tempting Alibi
Tempting Target
Tempting Trouble

ACKNOWLEDGMENTS

Thank you to Kari, Joan and Sarah for everything that you do! I'm also grateful to Jaycee with Sweet 'N Spicy Designs for her wonderful design work. Last but never least I owe a big thank you to my wonderful readers! Thank you guys for reading my books!

ABOUT THE AUTHOR

Savannah Stuart is the pseudonym of *New York Times* and *USA Today* bestselling author Katie Reus. Under this name she writes slightly hotter romance than her mainstream books. Her stories still have a touch of intrigue, suspense, or the paranormal and the one thing she always includes is a happy ending. She lives in the South with her very own real life hero. In addition to writing (and reading of course!) she loves traveling with her husband.

For more information about Savannah's books please visit her website at: www.savannahstuartauthor.com.

Printed in Great Britain
by Amazon